Anger!

To all children carried away in a whirlwind of anger.
You are good, and lovable, and full of wonderful energy!
G. T.

To my children and my goddaughters.
V.M.

To all the children I accompany as a coach
in the management of their emotions.
S.d.N.

Under the direction of Romain Lizé, President, MAGNIFICAT

Editor, MAGNIFICAT: Isabelle Galmiche
Editor, Ignatius: Vivian Dudro
Translator: Janet Chevrier
Proofreader: Kathleen Hollenbeck
Graphic Designers: Armelle Riva, Thérèse Jauze
Layout: Gauthier Delauné
Production: Thierry Dubus, Sabine Marioni

Original French edition: *Folle colère*
© 2018 by Mame, Paris
© 2021 by MAGNIFICAT, New York • Ignatius Press, San Francisco
ISBN Ignatius Press 978-1-62164-453-8 • ISBN MAGNIFICAT 9978-1-949239-58-4

how to
HANDLE MY
EMOTIONS

Anger!

THREE STORIES ABOUT
CHANNELING ANGER

Gaëlle Tertrais · Violaine Moulière · Ségolène de Noüel
Caroline Modeste

MAGNIFICAT · Ignatius

Contents

INTRODUCTION. 7

1. Tim Cheated!. 8

2. How Annoying!. 19

3. The Amusement Park 34

—————————————

What Have You Learned from These Stories? 46

The Pathway through Emotions 50

Parents' Corner. 52

Introduction

Of all the emotions, anger is the most powerful. If we let it boil over, it can cause real harm. But if we learn to channel anger, it can be a powerhouse for doing good.

In this book, you'll learn to recognize the early warning signs of anger: your cheeks are burning, your heart is racing, and your chest is tightening. You may even feel like shouting, lashing out, or smashing something. In this book, you'll also learn how to avoid doing these things, by keeping anger from overwhelming you.

Along with Elliot and Charlotte, you'll discover a whole toolbox of virtues to help you handle anger. You'll find out how to keep it in check, so that you can be happy by doing good and not harm.

And don't forget, God is ready to help you control your emotions. Whenever you turn to him in prayer or receive the sacraments of Communion or Reconciliation, God gives you his grace, which helps you to make the right choices.

1

Tim Cheated!

Driiiing!

At last, it was recess!

Tim and Elliot ran like lightning. The first one outside would get to start the game!

Everyone around them was excited, but Elliot kept his concentration. He was absolutely determined to win. He loved his favorite marble too much to lose!

He shot off his marble, and it rolled past the others. Now it was Tim's turn to aim. Elliot held his breath. Tim's marble came close to his. But, phew, it whisked by without touching it!

Tim ran up to check it. Looking as innocent as a lamb, he tapped it with his toe. Now the two marbles were touching each other.

"You lose, my friend! I got you!" declared Tim.

Elliot's blood boiled. He yelled, "You must be kidding. You cheated with your foot!"

Tim paid no attention. He just pocketed his winnings—Elliot's favorite marble.

Elliot shook with rage and clenched his teeth.

ELLIOT NOTICES HOW HIS BODY IS REACTING.

He threw himself at Tim, hitting him and screaming, "That's not fair! Give it back!"

Tim fought back. Now the two of them scrabbled on the ground, shouting, kicking, and punching in a cloud of dust.

Alerted by their shouts, a playground assistant ran up, took Elliot by the arm, and led him to stand by the playground fence.

"Hey, I'm not the one who cheated!" Elliot protested.

Tim, his hair in a tangle and his shirt hanging out, sneered at Elliot when the assistant's back was turned. That was the last straw! Elliot's anger boiled over.

Since he couldn't give Tim a whack, he started calling him nasty names at the top of his lungs.

"You rat! You cheater! You stupid idiot! You'll pay for this!" yelled Elliot.

The playground assistant brought Elliot inside to see his teacher, Mrs. Jones. Elliot struggled. Tears of rage and humiliation streamed down his cheeks.

"Oh my, how angry you are!" exclaimed Mrs. Jones. "Tell me what happened."

Between sobs, Elliot explained about the game and how Tim had cheated and stolen his

ELLIOT OWNS
HIS EMOTION.

favorite marble. He told how the playground assistant had done nothing to Tim but punished *him* instead.

Mrs. Jones listened very carefully. That helped. So Elliot went on, "I'm so, so angry!"

Mrs. Jones replied, "If Tim cheated, that's unfair, and it's normal for you to be angry. Anger is useful; it's a kind of messenger service!"

"I got the message all right," barked Elliot. "And I'm going to take my revenge!"

"Take your revenge?" Mrs. Jones said with surprise. "That's like setting a wildfire. Violence only brings more violence."

"But, then, what am I supposed to do?" asked Elliot in frustration.

"First, you need to understand that anger is neither good nor bad. It's what you decide to do with it that can be good or bad."

Mrs. Jones had Elliot's attention. "There are other options besides hitting," she continued. "Just now, you hit Tim. And what did that get you?"

"It felt good," Elliot replied.

"But did it get your marble back?" asked Mrs. Jones.

"No! And that's just not fair!"

ELLIOT RECOGNIZES HIS NEED FOR JUSTICE.

So hitting didn't solve the problem," Mrs. Jones reasoned. "Would you like me to suggest another way to deal with your anger?"

"Yes..."

"Let's try a game to put all this energy to use. I'll do it with you." Mrs. Jones stretched out one arm, with her hand straight up. "Blow on my hand as long as you can, and little by little I'll back away. With one deep breath, try to push me as far as the blackboard. Ready?"

TO RELEASE HIS ANGER, ELLIOT USES THE FIRST TOOL: BREATHING.

Elliot nodded, took a deep gulp of air and blew out in one breath.

"That's good," said Mrs. Jones. "Let's try again and see if we can go even farther."

Elliot took another deep breath and blew and blew until—Oof!—he couldn't blow any more. But Mrs. Jones was still a few steps away from the blackboard.

So Elliot breathed in again and blew, very gently, but for a very long time. That did it! Mrs. Jones was right up against the blackboard.

She smiled at him and said, "Bravo! How do you feel now?"

Elliot gave a sigh of relief. "I feel calmer now... more relaxed."

"When you do that," said Mrs. Jones, "the fire of your anger is still there. But little by little, it calms down without doing any damage. You temper it."

"*Temper it?*" asked Elliot.

"To temper means to reduce, to calm, to moderate. It's what gives us the word *temperance*—self-control. It can really help us when we're angry! It helps us to talk things over without getting upset."

As everyone came back in after recess, the classroom was suddenly full of activity. Among his classmates, Elliot spotted Tim. Elliot's heart began beating fast; he clenched his fists. Then, Elliot thought things over.

ELLIOT CONSIDERS.

Do I take revenge and stir up the fire? he asked himself. Or do I learn to be a firefighter? For a moment, Elliot wasn't sure. So he decided to take a deep breath. Then another. Elliot began to feel calmer.

"Mrs. Jones was right," he thought. "That breathing trick is helping."

During the whole math lesson, Elliot wondered how he could get his marble back. He could still feel his anger, burning like a little flame. Did he really want to put it out? Elliot hesitated.

Time passed. When the lunch bell rang, Elliot felt ready to talk to Tim without hitting him.

ELLIOT OPTS
FOR THE VIRTUE
OF TEMPERANCE.

On the playground, Mrs. Jones and Elliot walked over to Tim. Their teacher asked each of them to explain what had happened during

the game. Tim began to tell his view of the events, but he left out how he really won the marble. Elliot took a deep breath to keep himself calm.

After a few questions, Tim finally admitted that he had tapped the marble with his toe. Then, pretending it was no big deal, he handed the marble back to Elliot, saying, "Now we're even."

Elliot couldn't believe it! He'd gotten his marble back without having to punch Tim in the nose—just by talking to him, very simply. He was really pleased!

The fire inside him was now no more than a flicker. He could feel it gently going out.

Elliot looked at the sun glinting on his marble. That little marble had allowed him to see that anger doesn't necessarily have to go hand in hand with violence. He had tempered his anger! For first time in his life, he had put out its blazing fire!

During the afternoon, Mrs. Jones announced to the class, "Today, I'm going to talk to you about a great figure, Saint Teresa of Calcutta. When this woman arrived in India, she was deeply shocked by the poverty, by so many starving children and dying people abandoned in the streets. A great fire of anger burst in her heart. 'This isn't right!' she thought. 'People need to be loved, not neglected like this!' Mother Teresa wanted to make the world a better place. Do you think she used violence?"

Charlotte gave a chuckle and said, "Oh no, I can't imagine her even giving someone a nasty look!"

Everyone burst out laughing.

"No, I can't either!" said the teacher. "She thought about it and asked God what to do with all her fiery energy. Then she heard his answer: she must roll up her sleeves and start taking care of these suffering people herself. And that's just what she did! And many men and women joined her. Together they reached out with love and helped thousands of people!"

The whole class listened, wide-eyed. Mrs. Jones continued. "You see, anger can be an extraordinary engine to make the world a better place." With a little wink at Elliot, she added, "You, too—you can turn your anger into a force for good!"

To overcome his anger, Elliot used the virtue of temperance, which keeps us from doing harm and puts a brake on our overreactions.
Mother Teresa used the virtue of justice, which is love and respect for God and others. We are acting with justice when giving each person his due, including showing mercy toward those who suffer.

2

How Annoying!

Ripppp!

Charlotte caught herself on the door handle, and now her sparkly T-shirt was torn!

Oh no! She had counted on wearing it to Chloe's birthday party. Well, she could forget that now!

"Here, take that, you stupid door handle!"

Charlotte gave the door a good kick when suddenly—*Ka-boom!*—a thunderclap. Within seconds, black clouds covered the sky and rain began beating on the roof. Charlotte gasped. Unbelievable! Now her friend's outdoor birthday party would be cancelled! The invitation had warned: "In the event of rain, the party will be postponed."

Charlotte felt her temper mounting. She twisted her torn T-shirt in her hands.

From the top of the stairs, she yelled, "Daaady! Will the rain stop soon?"

"No, sweetheart, it doesn't look like it. Chloe's mom just phoned to say the birthday party is cancelled!"

Between clenched teeth, Charlotte muttered, "What a rotten day! It's raining cats and dogs, and now I'm stuck inside! Rats!"

Black clouds were gathering in her head as well. Then she had an idea that could change everything!

"Daaady? Daddy dear?"

Her father could see where this  was going. He replied with an amused smile, "Yes, sweetheart. Is there something you want to ask me?"

With a pout, Charlotte told him she was terribly upset and couldn't take any more. She had torn her favorite T-shirt, which was very annoying, and now the rain had ruined the party and any chance of playing outside. And... and...

"And...?"

"And I'd really like to play with my friend Elliot on our online video game!"

Charlotte's father thought it over. Charlotte could see he wasn't crazy about the idea. So, batting her eyelids at him, she pleaded, "Oh, pleeeease... Pretty pleeeease... Daddy..."

"Well, all right. But only for a half hour."

"Okay, I promise! Thank you! You're the best daddy in the world!"

Elliot's parents agreed too. Yippee! Elliot could play from his home at the same time as Charlotte. They would work as a team to dis-

cover the hidden treasure on a mysterious island. Hooray for video games! In Charlotte's mind, she was already there.

She was so excited that she could barely hear father's voice calling, "I'll set the timer to go off in thirty minutes. When it goes off, that's the end of the game, okay?"

"Okay..."

Charlotte turned on the video game and grabbed the remote control. She saw Elliot's pirate appear on the screen in a big black hat with a gilt saber slung across his chest. Her player joined him, jumping from rock to rock. She was dressed in a beautiful leopard-skin dress. We're off! The treasure map was a little torn and singed in places, but it was clear to see where the treasure was: in an underwater cave in Parrot Lagoon.

They would have to get through a forest full of monkeys who were already after them! Charlotte quickly pushed one into the water before he could snatch the map. The head monkey came swinging down on a vine, but Elliot cut him down with one slash of his sword. They ran, they jumped, and they dodged! Phew! They managed to scatter them all! But then Elliot fell into a mantrap. He was covered in leaves at the bottom of a pit. In the blink of an eye, Charlotte tied one end of a rope around a banana tree and tossed the other end down to Elliot. He had almost climbed all the way back up when—

Driiiing!

What?! Not already!! Charlotte decided to ignore her father's timer. She didn't care! She kept going, concentrating on hoisting up Elliot. But her father came and stood in front of the screen. Charlotte couldn't see anything! She felt her blood boiling and her heart beating fast. "Why can't Daddy get out of the way?!" she thought angrily.

Charlotte begged, "Daddy, no, really! Elliot's going to fall back down if we stop now! Just five more minutes, please! Five minutes!"

Her father grumbled but gave in.

"Okay," he said. "But," looking her straight in the eye, "in five minutes, you turn it off."

"Okay," Charlotte agreed, trying to look around him to see if Elliot was still in the pit.

Elliot was all right. He had even been able to pick up a coconut. They would need their strength to cross the enchanted bridge, because it was full of traps and pitfalls and swung if you tried to go too fast. You had to jump across missing planks. Should they slip, there were crocodiles awaiting them below! Charlotte got going again, but then—Yikes!—she slipped on a banana skin. Elliot caught her by the hand, but there she was, hanging in midair! She could see the great, gaping jaw of a crocodile just below her feet—

 Driiing!

 "Too bad for Daddy and his horrid timer!" she thought. "My life is at stake!"

"Charlotte?! Either turn it off now or I will!"

Charlotte's father was calling her, but she was hypnotized before the screen and tuned him out. Elliot took the coconut and threw it into the crocodile's jaws: he had saved her! She could at last climb back onto the bridge and—

And nothing. The screen had gone black. Charlotte's father was holding the electric plug.

"We agreed to five more minutes! You didn't turn it off, so I did it for you!"

CHARLOTTE NOTICES HOW HER BODY REACTS.

Charlotte could feel the anger rising up in her, real anger! In two seconds, she was filled with rage. She started shouting as loud as the thunder outside:

"You are mean! You ruined my game!"

With all her might, she threw down the remote control, which shattered into pieces. "So what if it's broken!" she shouted. "I don't care. I can't even play a game in this horrible family!"

Charlotte's father caught her with both hands and held her still.

"That's enough, Charlotte! Just because you're angry doesn't mean you can break things and be rude!"

She shot him a black look, wrestled free, and ran upstairs, knocking over the coat rack on her way. Charlotte slammed her bedroom door. Then she took her T-shirt and pulled hard at the tear. "There!" she said with triumph. "Now it's completely ripped, and I don't care!"

Soon, she heard her father knocking at the door, asking if he could come in.

"No! Go away!" she yelled. "I never want to see you again!"

Hearing his footsteps moving away, Charlotte flopped on the bed and began to cry. "What a completely rotten day," she thought. "Everything has gone wrong."

Charlotte was really, really angry...

The endless rain was still trickling down the windowpane when Charlotte dozed off, exhausted.

Tap, tap, tap.

There was her father again. In a sleepy voice, she whimpered, "Hmmm? What is it?..."

Charlotte felt the mattress squish down when her father sat next to her. He just sat there without speaking.

After a moment, she said to him, "Now I'll never get to finish my game!"

"I understand. And that's exactly why I let you play for five more minutes. And we agreed. But I think it would take you all day and night to finish that game."

"No way! Well, not all night anyway..."

"Yes, it would, because those games are made to go on and on, and that's why we need limits: to help us know when to stop!"

"Maybe, but it's too hard to stop! I can't do it; it makes me want to smash things."

"It's true; it's hard to stop. I can tell by your anger! But can you see the damage giving in to your anger has caused?"

Charlotte looked down. "Yeah, the remote. That was wrong to do...And I ripped my T-shirt even more.

"You know, it's possible to control that destructive energy. It takes effort and training. But I might have something to help you."

"Really?" Charlotte asked. "What?"

Her father took out his smartphone and suggested that he film her saying: "I, Charlotte, hereby promise to obey the limit and to stop when the set time for playing is up!"

"Why not?" Charlotte thought. She got up, stood at attention, and pronounced this solemn promise!

Then, on her own, she added, "And if that makes me angry, I promise not to destroy things!"

Then Charlotte's father suggested that she try again: go back to her game for fifteen minutes and to finish it very simply, by obeying!

"Really?!... But what about the remote?" she added glumly.

Her father stuck his hand in his pocket and pulled out the repaired remote. With a little wink, he explained, "This repair seemed a little too complicated for you. On the other hand, you should be able to put all the coats back where they belong!"

Charlotte threw herself into his arms. What a fantastic father she had!

Charlotte ran down the stairs, hung up all the coats, and clicked on her game. Elliot was still there! He had gotten far into the island. They were getting close to the underwater cave. They dove into a lagoon full of piranhas! Fortunately, they chased them away with their spears...

A dolphin swam in front of them to guide them to the tunnel leading to the cave with the treasure. There was lots of seaweed blocking the entrance, and they hadn't much oxygen left. What to do? To one side, she saw a place to get more air! Quick!

Driiing!
Charlotte growled. "Oh no! Not that again!"
She was about to start complaining when she heard her own voice in her head: "I, Charlotte, hereby promise..."

CHARLOTTE STOPS TO THINK.

CHARLOTTE CHOOSES THE VIRTUE OF OBEDIENCE.

She turned her head and saw herself on her father's smartphone. Her fingers itched; a storm was brewing inside her! She stopped to think.

"What do do?" she wondered. Shout and smash things? Or contain her anger and obey? "Yes, I want to change," she decided, and she had promised to obey the time limit she and her father had agreed upon.

To give herself strength, Charlotte took a deep breath and raised her hand in salute like a soldier.

She said to her father, "Aye, Aye, Captain!" Then she got up and turned off the game.

CHARLOTTE PRACTICES THE VIRTUE OF OBEDIENCE.

Oof! Charlotte felt better already. She could look her father in the eyes. She hadn't smashed or destroyed anything.

Suddenly, a beautiful ray of sunlight shone through the window. The storm had passed, and Charlotte had succeeded! It was true that she and Elliot still hadn't found the hidden treasure, but she had just found something even better: the treasure of obedience instead of violence. She could now handle her anger all by herself!

To overcome her anger, Charlotte used the virtue of obedience, which allows us to respect good and fair rules that have been set down and agreed to.

3

The Amusement Park

If there's one place Elliot really loves, it's the amusement park! When his parents said they were taking him there, he was really excited. He was bouncing all over the house! What's more, his parents had invited Charlotte too. Elliot was sure it was going to be a great day.

As soon as they arrived, his eyes were gleaming. The big Ferris wheel was turning round, huge and dizzying! The music made him want to dance. Everywhere, there were balloons and sparkling lights, and the aroma of cotton candy tickled his nose! He couldn't decide what to do first: the roller coaster or the bumper cars? The bumper cars! But then he spotted the dart game. He had always wanted to try his hand at darts! While Elliot's parents took his little brother to the bumper cars, he dragged Charlotte with him.

"You'll see; I've got better aim than you!" said Charlotte laughing.

"Want to bet?" asked Elliott.

"Yahoo!" he shouted as they arrived at the booth. "Just watch me win a prize the first time around!"

"Go on, I'll be nice. You go first," said Charlotte with a wave of her hand.

"Thanks!"

But there was just one problem: there were two people already ahead of them. Elliot fell in behind them when suddenly a boy much bigger than he, in a black leather jacket and a cap with a skull and crossbones, cut in front of him with a shove. Elliot was just about to say something when the big boy gave him such a mean look, the words stuck in his throat.

Elliot could feel the heat rising from the pit of his stomach to the tips of his ears.

ELLIOT NOTICES
HOW HIS BODY IS
REACTING.

36

Fire! Fire! His cheeks were burning. Soon he would have smoke coming out of his ears!

Overwhelmed by an enormous, monstrous anger, Elliot clenched his fists!

ELLIOT OWNS HIS EMOTIONS.

Elliot wanted to punch the back of that black jacket. But the boy scared him—especially with that skull and crossbones on his cap. Elliot knew it: if he moved an inch, that guy would beat him to a pulp. So he dropped his fists. He went limp, like a rag doll. And Elliot suddenly felt like crying.

Charlotte's voice brought him back to his senses. "Hey! Elliot! That guy's unbelievable!" she whispered. "You're not going to let him cut in front of you like that, are you?!"

"But you can see how big he is!" he replied with tears of rage. "He'd beat me to shreds in seconds!"

"I don't care how big he is. He's got no right to push ahead of you! Stand up for yourself!"

Suddenly they heard a cheer. A girl in pigtails got a bull's-eye on the first try. She chose a stuffed panda for her prize. The boy in the leather jacket then moved up to the booth.

"It should be my turn now," Elliot thought.

ELLIOT RECOGNIZES HIS NEED TO BE SHOWN RESPECT.

The man running the booth hadn't seen anything unusual and was about to hand the boy some darts. "He should pay more attention!" thought Elliot, wanting to yell at the man too.

"Here I am, so angry that I am not doing anything to stop that boy!" thought Elliot, feeling completely powerless. Quickly, he considered.

"I must be brave," he thought.

ELLIOT CHOOSES THE VIRTUE OF COURAGE.

Now determined, Elliot stamped his feet on the ground—*Thump! Thump!*—as he walked up to the man running the stand.

TO RID HIMSELF OF ANGER, ELLIOT USES A TOOL: HE STAMPS HIS FEET.

"Please, sir," shouted Elliot, a bit louder than he'd intended, "it's not his turn! It's my turn! He cut in front of me!"

ELLIOT PUTS COURAGE INTO PRACTICE.

39

The man looked from one to the other, from Elliot to the big boy in the black jacket.

"Is that right?" he asked.

"Well... yeah, I guess," said Elliot, losing his nerve.

The man immediately understood the situation. He asked the big boy to respect others by waiting in line for his turn like everyone else. And he gave the darts to Elliot instead.

Wow! It had worked! Elliot was relieved! His anger fell as flat as a pancake. He could hear the big boy grumbling behind him, muttering under his breath. Elliot tried to ignore him.

With fire in his veins, he shot the first dart and missed the target.

"Ha!" scoffed the boy behind him.

Elliot took a deep breath and aimed again. This time he hit a colored inside ring. He took another deep breath, and with the third dart, he hit the bull's-eye.

"Hooray!" shouted Charlotte, who hopped about, clapping with glee. Elliot pulled her by the arm and stood her between himself and the bully.

"Do you mind?" Elliot asked him. "She was right behind me in line. It's her turn now."

The boy was at a loss for words. He stepped back and let Charlotte have her turn. "He's being nice," thought Elliot. "He's not nasty after all." Elliot didn't feel like punching him anymore.

Charlotte looked at Elliot and whispered a little thank you. She took her three darts and hit the bull's-eye on the second try. She chose a rubber sword for her prize, while Elliot chose a flashlight.

As they walked away, Charlotte laughed and slashed the air with her toy sword.

"Why did you choose that for your prize?" Elliot asked.

Suddenly, she stopped and pointed the sword right at Elliot, saying in a solemn air: "Elliot, I dub you knight of the darts! And since you so bravely vanquished the dragon in the black leather jacket, I name you grand master of anger!"

They burst out laughing and ran to rejoin Elliot's parents at the bumper cars, where his little brother was having a great time. With a big smile of pride, Elliot showed his mom and dad what he had won.

"Well done!" his father congratulated him.

And, yes, Elliot was truly proud of himself. Not only because he had hit the bull's-eye but

because he had stood up for himself without becoming violent. He was proud of himself for using his anger to do something brave and to win respect.

"It's true," he thought, "I deserve respect!"

~~~~~~

Elliot used the virtue of courage to allow him to confront a scary, difficult situation.

~~~~~~

WHAT HAVE YOU LEARNED FROM THESE STORIES?

ANGER IS:
(Check the best answer.)

☐ a nasty failing   ☐ an emotion

Anger is often said to be a nasty failing. But anger is neither good nor bad. It's an emotion that arises whether you want it to or not. It's what you do with anger that's good or bad—for you and for others.

DID YOU KNOW?

There are many words to describe anger and its different degrees. Some are: annoyed, upset, irritated, infuriated, fuming, enraged.

ANGER SENDS A MESSAGE. IT TELLS YOU WHAT YOU NEED, WHICH MIGHT BE:

– respect
– justice
– to be listened to

– for your feelings to be respected
– to blow off steam

Think about the last time you felt angry. Finish the sentence below.

The last time I felt angry, anger told me that I needed

If we don't manage our anger and don't deal with our need, we remain stuck in that emotion. We are cut off from others who don't necessarily understand our anger. We can be trapped in negative thoughts and feelings that could lead to our saying and doing harmful things that we'll later regret.

WHAT TOOLS DO ELLIOT AND CHARLOTTE USE TO HANDLE THEIR ANGER?

Check the correct answers.
Look back at the stories to help yourself remember!

- ☐ Elliot uses his breathing to regain his calm and to talk instead of striking out.
- ☐ Charlotte stands at attention.
- ☐ Elliot stamps his feet on the ground to reaffirm himself and dare to retake his rightful place.
- ☐ Charlotte does a handstand.
- ☐ Elliot breathes flames.
- ☐ Elliot closes his eyes to concentrate.

VIRTUES COME
TO THE AID OF EMOTIONS!

In each story, Elliot and Charlotte choose a virtue to overcome their anger,

A virtue is a habit of choosing to do what is right. At first, that takes effort. But with time, it becomes easier and easier... a little like learning to ride a bike!

For example, you might say: "If I get used to obeying, little by little, it becomes natural. I'll feel less anger when I'm asked to turn the computer off. (It won't seem unfair to me anymore)."

CIRCLE THE VIRTUES THAT ARE USED IN THE STORIES IN THIS BOOK.

Courage

Prudence

TEMPERANCE STRENGTH

Obedience

Intelligence

Gluttony

PEACEFULNESS Justice

Diligence BULLYING

 SPOTLIGHT ON TEMPERANCE

Temperance is a virtue we all need when we get angry. It helps us restrain ourselves when we want to lash out. Temperance is also a virtue we need when we feel greedy, wanting too much of something. It could be too much food or too many toys or possessions. We need to restrain ourselves then, too, and temperance is the virtue that helps us put on the brakes!

THE PATHWAY THROUGH EMOTIONS

An emotion is a reaction to an event perceived by our five senses. It tells us we need something. Then it's up to us to work through it! To better understand what's happening, follow Elliot and Charlotte along the pathway of emotions!

I OWN MY EMOTION.

I ACT

So now, how do I deal with my emotion? Let's break it down into steps.

1. EXPERIENCING A STIMULUS
I hear someone's words or sense an unpleasant attitude. (Perhaps they impose limits, are physically aggressive, or insult me).
I experience an event (such as a setback, difficulty, or injustice).

2. SENSING MY EMOTIONAL REACTION
I sense: my heart racing, my face burning, my muscles tensing, and so on.
I feel: agitated, ready to explode, enraged, and the like.

3. IDENTIFYING THE EMOTION
I ask myself: What's happening to me?
I realize: I feel angry.

4. OWNING THE EMOTION
I own the emotion for what it is: neither good nor bad.

HOW WILL I HANI MY EMOTION?

8. MAKING A DECISION
I choose an attitude to take:
I will talk instead of hitting; I will accept the rules; I will dare to stand up for myself.

9. TAKING ACTION
I use the tools that will help me progress: breathing, standing at attention, or stamping my feet on the ground.

10. PRACTICING DAY AFTER DAY

10

HAPPINESS
Love, peace, joy, respect, self-worth, and so on.

TEMPTATION

REGRET

9

8

UNHAPPINESS
Holding a grudge, hatred, frustration, uneasiness, and so on.

How will I handle my emotion?

6

I STOP TO THINK...

5. DISCERNING WHAT TO DO
I think about what's really good for me and others.

6. RECOGNIZING MY NEED
I identify the need that prompted my anger. Perhaps I need to let off steam, to be treated kindly, or to demand justice.

5

VICE OR VIRTUE ?

7. LOOKING FOR A MEANS TO RESPOND TO MY NEED.
Virtues: Obedience, justice, temperance, courage
Vices: Disobedience, injustice, outbursts, cowardice

From their earliest years, children are able to identify specific emotions and, from the age of reason, they have the capacity to deal with it. This unique series on the emotions responds to that potential with both faith and guidance, offering a **virtuous** pathway to a happy life.

As a parent, teacher, or educator, how do you most often react to a child's angry outburst? Do you ask him or her to calm down? Do you feel your own anger rising and lose your temper? Do you simply ignore the tantrum?

THE TRIED-AND-TRUE APPROACHES IN THIS BOOK CAN HELP YOU FIND A BETTER WAY.

What is anger?

On one hand, anger is a disagreeable emotion that is, above all, frowned upon by others. It can rise up suddenly and powerfully, generating a surge of energy that can transform into violence harmful to oneself and to others.

And yet, anger is a healthy reaction to injustice, frustration, or aggression. It puts us in defense mode and gives us the energy to find what it is that we need. Sometimes, anger allows us to make ourselves noticed because we need attention or help in some way.

There are unhelpful expressions of anger.

Breaking things, hitting, rolling on the ground, screaming—all of these are violent manifestations of anger. We speak about "exploding with anger" or "being wild with rage" or "burning with fury."

How can you help a child through anger?

• Be there for the child.
Stop what you're doing and tend to the child. Anger can be dangerous for the person acting on it and for

others. So don't wait to step in. Bend down to the child's height but give him some space.

Speak firmly—in a loud voice, if necessary—but with kindness: "Oh my, you're really upset, aren't you? What's happened? Tell me about it."

• Listen.

Invite the child to tell you what he or she is feeling and to put a name to the emotion. If the child replies by shouting, crying, or speaking in disjointed sentences, listen carefully. Don't interrupt or try to correct the child, even if you can't understand everything he or she is saying. Remember that this young person is overwhelmed by a strong force spilling out. That's important; the release gives some relief.

If the child is physically lashing out, protect yourself, and protect others or objects nearby. Remain firm and calm, and protect the child from harm as well.

• Recognize the need.

Help the child to identify what it is that he or she needs. Perhaps it is justice, to be respected, to be accepted, or to let off steam.

In our stories, we see such examples. Elliot is very angry when Tim cheats at marbles; he needs justice. Charlotte is frustrated that she has to stop her video game; she needs her desire to be understood. At the amusement park, Elliot needs his turn in line to be respected.

SHOW UNDERSTANDING AND KINDNESS.

Always make the distinction between the anger and the reason for this emotion. The child's anger is legitimate—it's what he or she feels!—and you can't judge it, even if the reason for this anger doesn't seem justified to you. Avoid making trivial remarks such as, "Calm down!" or "Gently!" or "Stop!"

ANGER:
EMOTION OR SIN?

We use the word "anger" for both an emotion and a sin. But, emotion is morally neutral (neither good nor bad), while sin is a bad action. It's easy to confuse them. We don't have to feel guilty when anger rises within us; we haven't caused it! On the other hand, we are responsible for what we do with it. Anger (or wrath) is one of the seven deadly sins (or habitual dispositions to evil), along with pride, gluttony, lust, envy, sloth, and greed. They are called cardinal or capital sins because they can lead to a multitude of other sins. To combat them, God arms us at Baptism with the grace of the three theological virtues (faith, hope, and charity). We strengthen these and grow in the four cardinal virtues (prudence, temperance, fortitude, and justice) through prayer and the sacraments of Communion and Reconciliation.

• Promote responsibility

You are the child's guide, but you can't act on his or her behalf. Help the child to decide what can be done to get past the anger by calling on his or her intelligence, willpower, and courage. Help the child to understand that what's most important in the situation is to distinguish between what he or she feels and what he or she does. Ask: "What consequences might (or did) your anger have on others, on belongings, on yourself?" "What is it you would like to happen?" and "What do you think is a possible outcome?"

Once a positive step is selected, be sure the child feels responsible for the good choice he has made and support it.

• Go one step further

Be mindful of your own habits. How do you handle your anger? For example, do you yell at bad drivers who cut you off? In the heat of the moment, do insults burst from your lips? If your answer is yes, ask yourself: Does that do any good? Yelling and insulting others is neither a healthy habit nor a productive one. The more you let this habit take hold, the more you sink into a negative state of mind—and the harder it is to stop.

As a family, try to replace insults with kind words. Attend Mass together. And pray together at bedtime for the grace you need to grow in virtue.

With the help of God's grace, everyone in the family can practice more kindness, and even learn to bless and to pray for those who cause annoyance and pain.

Wishing someone well, whether friend or foe, and forgiving bring peace to our hearts and to those around us.

The example of Saint Teresa of Calcutta (page 15) teaches us to take strength from the energy anger gives us to do good.

And don't forget:

The path of virtue opens us to others and brings happiness!

Printed in August 2022 by Graphycems, Spain.
Job number MGN 22031
Printed in compliance with the Consumer
Protection Safety Act, 2008